Are You right for HIM?

Is HE right for YOU?

FUN QUIZZES About YOU & That Guy!

To Erin, Caitlin, and Eleni

By Catherine Daly-Weir

Grosset & Du

Copyright ©1999 by Catherine Daly-W
Grosset & Dunlap, Inc., a member of P
New York. GROSSET & DUNLAP is a tr
Published simultaneously in Canada. Printed in the U.S.A.
ISBN 0-448-41985-8   A B C D E F G H I J

TABLE OF CONTENTS

Are You Right for Him?
Is He Right for You?

Fun Quizzes About You & That Guy!

How to Use This Book:

Maybe the two of you have been dating for a couple of months now . . . maybe he just asked you out . . . or maybe you don't really know him, but the way he lights his Bunsen burner in chem class sends shivers down your spine. . . . No matter where your relationship stands, this book is for you! It's a fun, easy way to find out whether the two of you were meant to be, or if you're just two ships passing in the hallway.

Here's how! These quizzes are designed to determine how well you really know each other, how you feel about certain issues, what you have in common, etc. And each quiz comes in two parts—yours (You Say) and his (He Says). Answer part one yourself and see how you score. Next is when the real fun starts. You can either have him answer part two himself, or you can answer (honestly—not the way you'd want him to answer!) for him. Then add up your scores and find out how you two rate. Or, if you are truly flying solo at the moment—just do the girl part for now and save the boy section for later, when Mr. Might-Be-Right comes along. Hey—to paraphrase the Girl Scouts' motto: It never hurts to be prepared!

Do You Know the Real Him?
Does He Know the Real You?

Take the quiz on this page.
Then give the "He Says" part to your main man.
Compare your answers and find out
how well you two really know each other!

You Say

1 **The actress I think I most resemble in personality is:**
a) Sarah Michelle Gellar.
b) Gwyneth Paltrow.
c) Jennifer Lopez.

2 **The male movie star I most admire is:**
a) Matt Damon.
b) Will Smith.
c) Leonardo (no last name needed).

3 **For my birthday, the perfect gift would be:**
a) For him to throw me a surprise party with all my friends.
b) For him to take me out for a romantic dinner.
c) To receive the gift of Au—that's gold to those of you who haven't taken chemistry yet.

4 **I would probably get him a _____ for his birthday.**
a) diving watch
b) book of poetry
c) leather jacket

5 **You're entering the Biosphere for one year and you can take only one of the following videos with you. Which do you choose?**
a) *Scream.*

b) *The Wedding Singer.*
c) *Titanic*, of course.

6 Which of the following foods would you be *least* likely to sample at a salad bar?
a) Olives.
b) Blue cheese.
c) Three-bean salad.

7 If he were marooned on a desert island and a cooler full of candy bars washed up on shore, he would most want it to be loaded with _____.

8 Rank the following activities in order from your favorite to least favorite:
_____ Going to a movie with friends.
_____ Reading the latest book from Oprah's Book Club.
_____ Playing a video game.

9 If I were to hazard a guess, his all-time favorite sports star would have to be _____.

He Says

1 The actress I like best is:
a) Sarah Michelle Gellar.
b) Gwyneth Paltrow.
c) Jennifer Lopez.

2 The male movie star I resemble most in personality is:
a) Matt Damon.
b) Will Smith.
c) Leonardo.

3 For her birthday, I'd be most likely to:
a) Throw her a surprise party with all her friends.
b) Take her out for a romantic dinner.

c) Give her the gift of Au—that's gold to those of you who haven't taken chemistry yet.

4 Of the following, I would most like to get a _____ for my birthday.
a) diving watch
b) book of poetry
c) leather jacket

5 If your girlfriend had to pick one of the following videos, it would probably be:
a) *Scream.*
b) *The Wedding Singer.*
c) *Titanic.*

6 If you were planning a picnic for you and your sweetie, you know she'd just love you to pack some extra:
a) Olives.
b) Blue cheese.
c) Three-bean salad.

7 If you were marooned on a desert island and a cooler full of candy bars washed up on shore, you would most want it to be loaded with _____.

8 Rank the following activities in order from *her* favorite to least favorite:
_____ Going to a movie with friends.
_____ Reading the latest book from Oprah's Book Club.
_____ Playing a video game.

9 If I had to pick, my favorite sports star of all time would have to be: _____.

SCORING:
Add up all the answers you both got the same. Score two points for each matching answer. (No points for question #8 unless your ranking is totally correct.)

If your score is:

14–18: CLUED IN.
Wow! What a match! You probably finish each other's sentences, don't you? Just make sure you both have a few *outside* interests.

6–12: SOMEWHAT CLUELESS.
Well . . . maybe you like a little mystery in your relationships. Seriously, the two of you could just be lost in a romantic haze right now, but you should try to get to know each other's quirks and preferences a little better. You may even want to share a secret or two—it's fun!

0–4: COMPLETELY CLUELESS.
Hello? Do you at least know his/her name? Time to start paying a little more attention to each other!

Possession Is 9/10 of the Law!

Is it 100% of your relationship?
Do you want to own him?
Does he want to own you?
Take this quiz and find out!

You Say

1 How much time should a couple spend together?
a) I like to see him during the day and at least once on weekends, but if we have separate plans, that's okay.
b) I want to be picked up in the morning, escorted to every class, taken home, and he'd better not forget my good night phone call!
c) Uh, if a week or so goes by and we haven't touched base, I might start to wonder where he is.

2 You're at a party with your guy and you spot him across the room talking to another girl. So you:
a) Actually wouldn't even notice. You'd be too involved in your own conversation to be keeping tabs on him.
b) Shrug. He can talk to whomever he wants. (Unless it's that pom-pom girl who's been making googly eyes at him lately.)
c) Scream first, ask questions later. Yelling that his car is on fire is a great diversionary tactic.

3 Suppose the next thing you know, the two of them are nowhere to be found. When they reappear, twenty minutes later, you:
a) Hiss, "Take me home this instant, you lecherous pig."
b) Say, "Hey, where were you?"
c) Realize that he must have been showing her where the bathroom was. He is such a thoughtful guy!

4 True or false: I have bought (or have seriously con-

sidered buying) a sweatshirt for my sweetie that says "Property of _____."

(insert your name here)

Bonus point if you like it best when he wears it to the mall.

5 My guy has uttered the following lines to me: (Answer *always*, *sometimes*, or *never* to each statement.)

"Hey, cut me some slack."

"We're not Siamese twins, you know."

"I don't care how much you plead, I will *not* wear matching shirts!"

6 You're out on a double date with your best friend and her new boyfriend. Your friend tells a funny joke, and your boyfriend almost falls off his chair laughing. You're thinking:

a) I'll have to tell him about the time she had the whole schoolyard hysterical with her stand-up routine, "Take my teacher—please!"

b) I hope he thinks I'm funny, too.

c) It's too bad I'll never talk to her again; she was a really good friend.

7 You are surfing the net on your main man's laptop when the "You've Got Mail" icon starts flashing. The sender is an unfamiliar, definitely female name. So you:

a) Keep on surfing. It's illegal to tamper with the mail!

b) Ask him who "cutiepie@aol.com" is.

c) "Accidentally" open it. Maybe he'll never notice.

He Says

1 How much time should a couple spend together?

a) An average amount, I guess. And Saturday nights on most weekends.

b) What's the point of dating if we're not together as close to 24-7 as possible? And if we get separated, that's what our matching pagers are for.

c) When I can't remember what she looks like, it's time for another date.

2 **You and your beloved are at a party, and you see her across the room talking to another guy. So you:**

a) Smile. You are very lucky to have such a nice and friendly girlfriend!

b) Join in if you think it might be an interesting conversation, but she can talk to whomever she pleases. (Except for maybe her quarterback ex!)

c) Set off the guy's car alarm so he has to go outside to turn it off, killing the conversation.

3 **The next thing you know, the two of them are MIA. What's your reaction?**

a) Round up all your pals. We're going on a manhunt!

b) Worry she's swapping spit with Mr. Smoothie while you're looking like a geek by the punch bowl.

c) Trust is the name of your game, buddy. No questions asked.

4 **True or false: I have given my lady love a varsity jacket with my name emblazoned on it. Bonus point if you insist she wears it at all times.**

5 **The g.f. has uttered the following lines to me: (Answer *always*, *sometimes*, or *never* to each statement.)**

"Do you really have to call me three times a day?"

"Sometimes I feel a little bit . . . suffocated in this relationship."

"You tattooed my name *where*?!"

6 The two of you are hanging out with your best buddy, and your girlfriend admires his new jacket. You say:
a) "That's my man. He's always stylin'."
b) "Think I could borrow it?"
c) "Yeah, he looks good—when he remembers to shower."

7 Your girlfriend is sick and she asks you to bring some books home for her. While you are scouring her locker for her chem notebook, you unearth her journal. You would:
a) Put it back where it belongs.
b) Sneak a peek, just to see what she said about your date last Friday night.
c) Xerox it for future reference.

SCORING:
1) a=2 b=3 c=1
2) a=1 b=2 c=3
3) a=3 b=2 c=1
4) true=2 false=0
5) always=2 sometimes=1 never=0
   always=2 sometimes=1 never=0
   always=2 sometimes=1 never=0
6) a=1 b=2 c=3
7) a=1 b=2 c=3

If your score is:

18–24: MINE! MINE! MINE!
It's time to learn how to relax a bit. Unless your SO (Significant Other) has given you a valid reason not to be trusting, maybe you should cut him or her some slack. And if the SO finds out what you've been up to in the name of love, you may suddenly find yourself SO-less.

12–17: PLAYS WELL WITH OTHERS.
You are a wee bit possessive, but not alarmingly so. You tend to

keep it under control. If your score is a bit on the high side, you might want to watch the tendency toward unrealistic demands.

5–11: TAKE HIM/HER, HE/SHE'S YOURS.
There isn't a possessive bone in your body, is there? Good for you. Trust must be your middle name—but what were your parents thinking?

Couples Quotient:
Scoring differently on this quiz isn't necessarily grounds for immediate breakup, but it can be a problem when one person is super-possessive and the other has an I've-got-to-be-free attitude. The possessive one may feel slighted . . . and the not-too-possessive one may feel smothered!

The Perfect Prom

...is a term that means different things
to different people.
To some, it's the ultimate in romance.
To others, the only good prom
is the one they don't have to go to.
So let's find out if it means different things
to the two of you!

You Say

1 I picture myself at the prom wearing:
a) A strapless white gown with tulle skirt, and delicate white high heels. I reach up (with my professionally manicured nails) to straighten the bejeweled tiara that rests precariously upon the mountain of curls on my head.
b) A sleek black halter dress.
c) A vintage '50s prom dress with cat's-eye glasses.
d) Actually, the perfect prom-night attire would be my pajamas, but if I really have to go, I'll just wear the first thing I see in my closet.

2 The flowers I'd most like to receive from my man would be:
a) A wrist corsage of perfect pink rosebuds and baby's breath.
b) A single red rose.
c) One of those funny corsages that looks like a puppy's face.
d) A handpicked bunch of dandelions, please. Watch as I mock bourgeois prom traditions!

3 If I had to describe the prom in one word it would be:
a) Romantic. As Martha would say, it's a *good* thing.
b) Cool. We look great; what else matters?

c) Fun. Friends, music, punch. And as an added bonus I get to watch the teachers dance—that's always good for a laugh.

d) Painful. It's a twice-in-a-lifetime chance to see the gymnasium decorated with crepe paper. (As if the junior prom wasn't enough!)

4 My favored mode of transportation is:

a) A white stretch limo, the bigger the better.

b) The coolest convertible Rent-a-Clunker has to offer. (We are on a high-school budget, after all.)

c) To pile as many friends as possible into my mom's old Yugo and pray for green lights all the way there.

d) The Q44A. What are bus passes for, anyway, if not to take you to school functions?

5 Who would pay?

a) The boy, of course. That's why I love tradition so much!

b) The inviter.

c) We'd split it 50/50.

d) We'd crash when it's halfway over, and we've both got those bus passes, so this question is pointless.

6 The pre-prom meal would be:

a) A romantic candlelit dinner for two at the classiest French restaurant in town. I hear the *faux pas* is excellent.

b) We'd go out for sushi at the trendiest place around.

c) We'd go out for a family-style meal with all our friends and make sure that if one person eats the garlic bread, we *all* do.

d) Burger Mart. I hear they've got this great buy-one-get-one-free deal.

7 The theme for the perfect prom would be:

a) Some Enchanted Evening.

b) You Are the Dancing Queen.

c) Girls Just Wanna Have Fun.
d) We Gotta Get Outta This Place.

8 At the perfect prom, most of the dances would be:
a) Slow ones—the slower the better.
b) All the ones I do best, of course!
c) Free-for-all—I'd mosh the night away with all my friends.
d) A Conga Line—out the door.

9 The words I would most want to hear at the prom are:
a) "Will _____ and _____
        (insert his name here)   (insert your name here)
please make their way to the stage so they can be crowned King and Queen of the Prom?" from the emcee.
b) "You look marvelous!" from the best-dressed girl in school.
c) "No curfew. Just party all night with your friends!" from your mom as you walk out the door.
d) "We're extremely sorry for the inconvenience, but _____ appears to be in (insert name of your high school here)
the path of a rogue hurricane. The prom is canceled. Please return to your homes immediately," from the principal, who is sweating profusely.

He Says

1 I picture myself wearing:
a) A tuxedo, of course, with a cummerbund that matches my date's dress, and one of those cool ruffly shirts.
b) A Bond, James Bond-style tux.
c) A tux, but I must insist on wearing my Chucks with it.
d) If I really had to go I'd borrow a suit from my father/brother/uncle. They're all six inches shorter than me, but hey, who cares?

2 For a boutonniere, I'd prefer:
a) A single rosebud that perfectly matches my date's dress, naturally.
b) Whatever looks most striking against my tux.
c) Something colorful, I guess.
d) . . . not to have to wear a silly flower on my lapel, thank you very much.

3 If I had to describe the prom in one word it would be:
a) Romantic. As Martha would say, it's a *good* thing.
b) Cool. We look great; what else matters?
c) Fun. Friends, music, punch. And as an added bonus I get to watch the teachers dance—that's always good for a laugh.
d) Painful. It's a twice-in-a-lifetime chance to see the cafeteria decorated with crepe paper. (As if the junior prom wasn't enough!)

4 My favored mode of transportation is:
a) A white stretch limo, the bigger the better.
b) The coolest convertible Rent-a-Clunker has to offer. (We are on a high-school budget, after all.)
c) To pile as many friends as possible into my mom's old Yugo and pray for green lights all the way there.
d) The Q44A. What are bus passes for, anyway, if not to take you to school functions?

5 Who would pay?
a) The man (that's me) always pays.
b) Whoever issued the invite.
c) We'd split it 50/50.
d) We'd crash after the meal, and we've both got the aforementioned bus passes, so this question is pointless. Next!

6 The pre-prom meal would be:
a) A romantic candlelit dinner for two at the classiest

French restaurant in town. I hear the *faux pas* is excellent.

b) We'd go out for sushi at the trendiest place around.

c) We'd go out for a family-style meal with all our friends and I'd make sure if my date eats a piece of garlic bread, I eat *two*.

d) Burger Mart. I hear they've got this great buy-one-get-one-free deal.

7 **The theme for the perfect prom would be:**

a) Some Enchanted Evening.

b) Some Guys Have All the Luck.

c) Party Train.

d) We Gotta Get Outta Here Right Now.

8 **At the perfect prom, most of the dances would be:**

a) Slow ones—the slower the better.

b) All the ones I do best, of course!

c) Free-for-all—I'd mosh the night away with all my friends.

d) A Conga Line—out the door.

9 **The words I would most want to hear at the prom are:**

a) "Will _____ and _____

     (insert your name here)   (insert her name here)

please make their way to the stage so they can be crowned King and Queen of the Prom?" from the emcee.

b) "The girls in the theater club have unanimously elected you 'Lord of the Dance,'" from the cutest stagehand.

c) "No curfew. Just party all night with your friends!" from your mom as you walk out the door.

d) "We're extremely sorry for the inconvenience, but _____ appears to be in

(insert name of your high school here)

the path of a rogue hurricane. The prom is canceled. Please return to your homes immediately," from the principal, who is sweating profusely.

SCORING:

If your answers are mostly A's:
You are a prom traditionalist. Floor-length gown, tux with matching cummerbund, perfect flowers, limo—it just wouldn't be right if everything wasn't done to a T. You've probably been planning for the prom since the second grade, haven't you? Just don't get too caught up in the pressure to do everything right, and make sure to have a good time!

If your answers are mostly B's:
Admit it, you *are* into the prom, but maybe looking good is your first priority.

If your answers are mostly C's:
No need to take the prom seriously—it's all about fun for you! You do the prom on your own terms, traditions be darned!

If your answers are mostly D's:
You'll go—kicking and screaming, that is. And you probably wouldn't even do that if your mother didn't want those prom pictures for her album so badly, would you? Smile, say cheese, and act like you're having fun!

Couples Quotient:
If the two of you haven't scored the same, don't worry—most combinations can sort out their prom differences. But be afraid—be very afraid—if, say, you're a D and he's an A. He'll be smiling away for photos in his white tux and ruffly blue shirt, while you roll your eyes and wish you were back at school taking that physics final!

Style or Substance?

Face it—we all judge a book
by its cover once in a while.
But just how often do you two do it?

You Say

1 **Your friend tells you about this new guy she's met at her job at the animal shelter—he's sweet, has a great sense of humor, and (most important to her) is kind to animals. When you drop in to check out the latest batch of kittens, there he is—in all his taped-up-glasses-and-highwaters glory. You tell your friend:**
a) "I know love is blind, but geek-boy is ridiculous."
b) "If he makes you laugh, he's aces with me."
c) "He's, well, *different* than the other guys you've dated."

2 **A new family moves in next door with a son your age. You haven't seen him yet. When you ask your sister what the new boy is like, she says, "He's really very nice." Your reaction?**
a) Sis is a good judge of character. He must be a very nice guy.
b) But is he cute?
c) Thanks for nothing. That could mean *anything*.

3 **You find out that your mother's friend's daughter is transferring to your school. You have very fond memories of the time you spent together collecting ants when you were five, so you are psyched to see her again. But when your friends (not realizing you know the girl wearing the "SAVE THE DUNG BEETLES" T-shirt) say, "Check out Bug Girl," your reaction is to:**
a) Re-introduce yourself to her, but steer her toward the entomology club.

b) Start up where you left off. You forgot all about her wacky sense of humor!

c) Run the other way. You didn't cultivate your coolness quotient to see it destroyed in one fell swoop.

4 You're going sledding with your fella and some of his friends. You really want to make a good impression, so you put on your cutest hat-and-mitten set. Your footwear choices are an uninsulated yet fashionable pair of boots that totally match your ensemble or a goofy pair of worn but really warm hand-me-down duck boots from your big brother. You choose:

a) The ugly warm ones, though you feel like a complete geek.

b) High fashion, even if it means frostbite. Hey—you don't really need all ten of those toes anyway . . . .

c) There's no question—you'll wear whatever protects your tootsies from the elements, fashion be darned!

5 In English class your teacher has you choose partners to give a presentation on Shakespeare. Lucky you—two guys ask to be your buddy—Dexter Walsh and Jake Johnson. Each has his strengths—Dexter is wild for the Bard, and Jake has the most incredible blue eyes you have ever had the pleasure of staring into. Who do you choose?

a) Easy! Jake, 'cause he's so cute.

b) Easy! Dexter, so he can do all the work.

c) Easy! Dexter, because you'll learn a lot from him.

6 Be truthful here! You go to a school dance with your new beau. You head out to the dance floor and suddenly Cute Boy's moves are making Elaine from *Seinfeld* look like Janet Jackson. So you:

a) Smile and dance away. So what? He can't be good at *everything*.

b) Wince, but continue to dance. Rent *Dirty Dancing* and *Strictly Ballroom* on your next video night. Make him watch them twice.

c) Fake a sprained ankle and demand to be taken home.

7 Your boyfriend shows up at your house to go to your friend's party in a shirt that is hid-e-ola. We're talking neon green. You:

a) Put on a pair of sunglasses and head out the door. It's what's *in* the shirt that counts.

b) Refuse to go out until he has traded the shirt for an acceptable one of your brother's.

c) Use your formidable powers of suggestion throughout the evening so he won't take off his jacket. "Brrrr! It's freezing in here, don't you think?"

He Says

1 Your friend who generally has great taste in the ladies confesses that he has a crush on a girl in your English class. She's not exactly going to be elected Prom Queen. You:

a) Suggest a trip to the optometrist is in order.

b) Tell him she diagrams a mean sentence—he should go for it!

c) Say, "Who am I to stand in the way, *if you're sure about it.*"

2 You would feel ten feet tall if a friend of yours was to say your girlfriend was:

a) One of the most wonderful people he's ever met.

b) Totally hot.

c) Hysterically funny.

3 Your cousin is a nice guy with an encyclopedic knowledge of baseball, but he's, well, geekish. When you're at the mall with your buddies and you see him getting a foot-long at the Hot Dog Hut, you:

a) Say, "Hey guys, this is Lester." No mention of shared gene pool necessary.

b) Say, "Hey, this is my cousin Lester. He's a baseball genius! Ask him any player's batting stats—go ahead, anybody's!"

c) Go grab a taco instead.

4 Your girlfriend's dad scores some tickets to see your favorite football team play. That morning is bitterly cold. Your mom insists you wear earmuffs. You:

a) Stuff them in your pocket and put them on only when your girlfriend announces that your ears are so red they are going to fall off.

b) Leave them in the car so you won't be tempted to put them on during the game and look like a fool.

c) Wear them and—when those Arctic breezes are particularly stiff—also throw on that colorful pom-pom hat.

5 It's class election time, and the two candidates couldn't be more different from each other. Debbie Thurston's campaign posters feature an 8x10 photo of her fine self, but her only campaign promise is More Fat-Free Options at the cafeteria. Katie Holmes wants to allot more school funds to update the library and hold bake sales to raise money for widows and orphans. You vote for:

a) Debbie. She's cute.

b) Debbie. A few more fat-free options wouldn't be so bad, would they?

c) Katie. It would be really helpful if the library had more reference books. And how can you disappoint those poor little orphans?

6 You sense something is wrong when your cheerleader girlfriend is a little wobbly on her roundoff. So when she climbs to the top of the human pyramid, loses her balance, and lands in the vice principal's lap, you aren't terribly surprised. You are, however:

a) Concerned. You take her out for cheese fries and a Coke to soothe her bruised feelings.

b) Blasé. You meet her after the game and shrug. So she looked like an idiot. She'll get over it!

c) Humiliated. You leave the game immediately to avoid being seen with her. You'll resume your boyfriendly duties after this blows over.

7 Your lovely girlfriend gets hit in the face (à la Marcia Brady) with a softball during team practice and has a huge nose and two black eyes. It's two days before the Homecoming Dance. She says she still wants to go. You:

a) Buy her the biggest, most beautiful corsage you can find. What a trouper!

b) Insist that the two of you should stay home. You have to think of your image.

c) Go, but suggest you forego the photos this time around.

SCORING:

1) a=3 b=1 c=2
2) a=1 b=3 c=2
3) a=2 b=1 c=3
4) a=2 b=3 c=1
5) a=3 b=2 c=1
6) a=1 b=2 c=3
7) a=1 b=3 c=2

If your score is:

17–21: SUPER SUPERFICIAL.
It seems to be all style over substance for you. All you seem to care about is how you (and other people) look. Maybe it's time to stop caring so much about other people's opinions and start

judging yourself (and others) less harshly. Who knows—with your new attitude, you might even make some new friends!

12–16: SOMEWHAT SUPERFICIAL.

You try, but sometimes it is so hard not to give in to your shallow side. Keep on fighting the good fight. Remember how great it felt the times you let yourself stop worrying about what "they" thought about you?

7–11: SUPER DEEP.

You go girl/boy! It's not about looks or appearances for you. You judge people by a different (more discerning) set of rules.

Couples Quotient:

Super superficial and super deep may make for a difficult partnership. After all, marriage counselors tend to say that "shared values" make for a lasting relationship. Okay, okay—you're not married. But hey, it's something to think about.

It's a Matter of Time

Are you an early bird?
Ms./Mr. Punctuality?
A little late?
Or lost in space?
The clock is ticking . . . .
How well do you two match up?

You Say

1 **Suppose the last bell before first period rings at 8:17. At 8:16:55 where can you be found?**
a) Sitting in math class for five minutes now, and counting.
b) Standing outside your classroom, talking to a classmate.
c) In the hallway, frantically searching for your history notebook.
d) Sitting in the cafeteria, daydreaming. Where did everybody go?

2 **Your friend is planning a surprise party for her boyfriend. You know he's arriving at 3:00. What time do you get there?**
a) 2:00. You're not taking any chances of ruining the surprise.
b) 2:45. Plenty of time to duck behind the couch.
c) 3:10. Lucky for you, Birthday Boy is running late, too.
d) 4:00. Isn't that the time she said?

3 **Answer true or false to the following statements:**
a) My overdue library fines could lower property taxes for every man, woman, and child in town.
b) When making plans with me, I have noticed that my friends routinely subtract fifteen minutes from the actual time they want me to be ready.

c) I won the "Perfect Attendance Record" in elementary school.

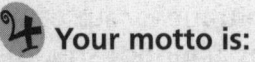 **Your motto is:**
a) The early bird gets the worm.
b) Better late than never, but better never late.
c) Better late than never.
d) Take time to smell the roses.

 **When you go to the movies:**
a) You're waiting outside before the previous movie ends.
b) You give yourself just enough time to go to the bathroom, get your popcorn, and pick out a good seat (in the middle of the aisle, about halfway back—no big hats or hair to obscure your line of vision).
c) You arrive just as that psychedelic lava screen shuts down (it makes you dizzy) and the coming attractions begin.
d) You're always confused when people talk about the opening credits. What are they anyway?

When your alarm goes off, you:
a) Are already in the shower.
b) Generally get up, though you may occasionally hit the snooze button.
c) Hit snooze once or twice—you rely on those extra zzzz's.
d) Turn over and go back to sleep.

You are meeting a friend on the corner of Smith and 9th at 3:30. After waiting fifteen minutes:
a) It's still only 3:15, so you're unconcerned.
b) It's 3:45, so you figure she must be running late.
c) It's 4:00, so you start to wonder if this is the wrong corner.
d) It's 4:30. Did you get the day wrong again?

8 In your school career you have amassed enough tardy slips to:
a) Tardy slip? I beg your pardon!
b) Make a paper airplane.
c) Line your cat's litter box.
d) Paper the entire auditorium.

He Says

1 Say the last bell before first period rings at 8:17. At 8:16:55 where can you be found?
a) Sitting in math class for five minutes now, and counting.
b) Standing outside your classroom, talking to a classmate.
c) In the hallway, frantically searching for your history notebook.
d) Sitting in the cafeteria, daydreaming.

2 Your friend is planning a surprise party for his girl-friend. You know she's arriving at 3:00. What time do you get there?
a) 2:00. You're not taking any chances of ruining the surprise.
b) 2:45. Plenty of time to duck behind the couch.
c) 3:10. Lucky for you, Birthday Girl is running late, too.
d) 4:00. Isn't that the time he said?

3 Answer true or false to the following statements:
a) My overdue library fines could lower property taxes for every man, woman, and child in town.
b) When making plans with me, I have noticed that my friends routinely subtract fifteen minutes from the actual time they want me to be ready.
c) I won the "Perfect Attendance Record" in elementary school.

4 Your motto is:
a) The early bird gets the worm.

b) Better late than never, but better never late.
c) Better late than never.
d) Take time to smell the roses.

5 When you go to the movies:
a) You're waiting outside before the previous movie ends.
b) You give yourself just enough time to go to the bathroom, get your popcorn, and pick out a good seat (in the middle of the aisle, about halfway back—no big hats or hair to obscure your line of vision).
c) You arrive just as that psychedelic lava screen shuts down (it makes you dizzy) and the coming attractions begin.
d) You're always confused when people talk about the opening credits. What are they anyway?

6 When your alarm goes off, you:
a) Are already in the shower.
b) Generally get up, though you may occasionally hit the snooze button.
c) Hit snooze once or twice—you rely on those extra zzzz's.
d) Turn over and go back to sleep.

7 You are meeting a friend to go shopping. You're supposed to meet on the corner of Smith and 9th at 3:30. After waiting fifteen minutes:
a) It's still only 3:15, so you're unconcerned.
b) It's 3:45, so you figure he must be running late.
c) It's 4:00, so you start to wonder if this is the wrong corner.
d) It's 4:30. Did you get the day wrong again?

8 In your school career you have amassed enough tardy slips to:
a) Tardy slip? I beg your pardon!
b) Make a paper airplane.
c) Line your cat's litter box.
d) Paper the entire auditorium.

SCORING:

1) a=3 b=2 c=1 d=0
2) a=3 b=2 c=1 d=0
3) a- true=0   false=2
   b- true=0   false=2
   c- true=2   false=0
4) a=3 b=2 c=1 d=0
5) a=3 b=2 c=1 d=0
6) a=3 b=2 c=1 d=0
7) a=3 b=2 c=1 d=0
8) a=3 b=2 c=1 d=0

If your score is:

21–27: SUPER EARLY.
You are obsessively early. People could set their watches by you—except they'd be fast!

14–20: ON TIME.
You are a pretty timely person. You hate to rush, so you usually leave yourself lots of leeway. Once in a while, you may miscalculate, but hey, nobody's perfect!

7–13: RUNNING LATE.
Ideally, you want to arrive on the dot and not a moment sooner. Which means you are routinely late. Honestly, don't you get tired of always rushing? Try setting your clock ten minutes fast, or not hitting that snooze button in the morning!

0–6: LOST IN SPACE.
Time has no meaning for you.

Couples Quotient:
This can be tricky! Chronic latecomers and early birds usually drive each other crazy! But maybe you two can be a good influence on each other. Say you're *always* early and he's not. You can set his watch fifteen minutes fast, and he can teach you how to relax a little!

How Romantic Are You?
How Romantic Is He?

Here's a fun way to find out.
Imagine you're writing to your main man.
Complete the letter by answering these questions.
Then let him imagine he's writing to you.
See which one of you is the biggest romantic!

You Say

1 Pick your favorite salutation:
a) Dear Sweetie,
b) Hey, You!
c) To the Light of My Life,

2 I can't go a _____ without you.
a) week or two
b) millisecond
c) day

3 When I'm not with you,
a) I'm pining away for you.
b) I'm looking forward to seeing you again.
c) I'm doing other things.

4 Today I saw a beautiful bird in the sky. It made me think:
a) I wish you were here to see it, too.
b) I hope it doesn't use me for target practice.
c) Like our love, it soars to the heavens on gossamer wings.

5 I was thinking about our upcoming anniversary.
a) When is it again?
b) I made reservations for a romantic dinner.
c) I thought we could recite poetry under the stars together.

6 The next time I see your mom, I want to:
a) Thank her for the gift of you.
b) Ask for her meat loaf recipe.
c) Ask her if it's okay if we stay out a little past curfew next Saturday.

7 There's a movie title that reminds me of our relationship. It's:
a) *As Good as It Gets*.
b) *Love Is a Many Splendored Thing*.
c) *Reality Bites*.

8 If I could get you anything, it would be:
a) Dental floss, the gift that keeps on giving.
b) A new bike, so you could always race over to see me.
c) The brightest star in the sky.

9 Pick your favorite closing:
a) Worshipfully yours,
b) Love,
c) See ya around sometime,

_____
(insert your name here)

He Says

1 Pick your favorite salutation:
a) Dear Sweetie,
b) Hey, You!
c) To the Light of My Life,

2 I can't go a _____ without you.
a) week or two
b) millisecond
c) day

3 **When I'm not with you,**
a) I'm pining away for you.
b) I'm looking forward to seeing you again.
c) I'm doing other things.

4 **Today I saw a beautiful bird in the sky. It made me think:**
a) I wish you were here to see it, too.
b) I hope it doesn't use me for target practice.
c) Like our love, it soars to the heavens on gossamer wings.

5 **I was thinking about our upcoming anniversary.**
a) When is it again?
b) I made reservations for a romantic dinner.
c) I thought we could recite poetry under the stars together.

6 **The next time I see your mom, I want to:**
a) Thank her for the gift of you.
b) Ask for her meat loaf recipe.
c) Ask her if it's okay if we stay out a little past curfew next Saturday.

7 **There's a movie title that reminds me of our relationship. It's:**
a) *As Good as It Gets*.
b) *Love Is a Many Splendored Thing*.
c) *Reality Bites*.

8 **If I could get you anything, it would be:**
a) Dental floss, the gift that keeps on giving.
b) A new bike, so you could always race over to see me.
c) The brightest star in the sky.

9 **Pick your favorite closing:**
a) Worshipfully yours,

b) Love,
c) See ya around sometime,

_____
  (insert your name here)

SCORING:

1) a=2 b=1 c=3
2) a=1 b=3 c=2
3) a=3 b=2 c=1
4) a=2 b=1 c=3
5) a=1 b=2 c=3
6) a=3 b=1 c=2
7) a=2 b=3 c=1
8) a=1 b=2 c=3
9) a=3 b=2 c=1

If your score is:

22–27: ROMEO & JULIET.
Are you for real? You are about as romantic and sentimental as a person can be.

15–21: HOMER & MARGE.
You are about average on the romance scale. You do care, and from time to time you'll make a gesture that gets your sweetie's heart fluttering. Of course, you could do it a little more often!

9–14: SISKEL & EBERT.
You're a little too practical about romance. Here's a tip—nobody appreciates the gift of dental floss, even if it does mean better oral hygiene.

Couples Quotient:
Of course, any mix could work. Opposites attract, they always say! But hopeless romantics might be just a little disappointed by someone who's not all that enthusiastic about matters of the heart.

Do You Speak First, Think Later? Does He?

Admit it, occasionally we all say
the first thing that pops into our minds.
But sometimes it's not the wisest thing to do.
Take this quiz and see if you (or he) does it TOO often.

You Say

1 **The boyfriend asks you if you think he's going to be bald like his dad. You answer:**
a) "Silly, everyone knows it's whether your mother's father was bald that determines your hair loss. . . . Oh, that's right, he's bald, too."
b) "Why are you worrying about something so unimportant? Besides, bald's not so bad—look at Michael Jordan!"
c) "Of course not." (Though frankly you'd be shocked if he isn't as bald as a Ping Pong ball in twenty years.)

2 **Your boyfriend is taking ceramics as an elective and is excited about his latest project. When he shows it to you, you're not quite sure if it's a paperweight, a sugar bowl, an ashtray, or none of the above. So you say:**
a) "Sweetie, your new nickname is Claymaster!"
b) "Wow! What a great glaze!"
c) "What in the world *is* this thing?"

3 **Your guy gets all domestic on you and bakes you some cookies. With your first bite it's apparent he left out at least one crucial ingredient. So you:**
a) Spit it out and say, "I appreciate the gesture, but maybe it's time to retire that apron."
b) Stuff your face with a big smile, even though you're going to have a killer stomachache later.
c) Offer him one and hope he notices something is amiss.

4 Your best friend asks you to go out on a double date with her and her boyfriend. The last time you doubled they ended up in a screaming match at The Rusty Fork and you were caught in the crossfire of flying dinner rolls. So you reply:

a) "Thanks, but I'm not in the mood to watch you two vie for the Nastiest Couple Award."

b) "Sorry, but we've got plans. Maybe some other time."

c) "Sounds great!" (Your boyfriend is going to kill you when he finds out!)

5 Surprise! Your guy gets you tickets to the circus for your anniversary. You despise the circus, and haven't been since you were five and were carried out of the Big Top screaming. So you:

a) Thank him for his thoughtfulness but suggest that he take his little cousin instead.

b) Squeal, "Ooh—I can't wait to see the clowns!" (Even though the red-nosed freaks secretly give you nightmares.)

c) Say, "Hello! Shows how much you know about me, Dumbo."

6 Your mom loves to come and cheer at your softball games, but lately her unsportswoman-like behavior (incessant screaming at the ump, harassing the opposing team) has you mortified. So you:

a) Smile and keep on pitching.

b) Take her aside and inform her that her habit of living vicariously through your achievements is transparent and embarrassing.

c) Ask her if something's been bothering her lately.

7 Your boyfriend informs you that he made a ten-dollar bet with his buddy that he will beat him in a tennis match. His buddy just happens to be the captain of the tennis team. You say:

a) "I'm very impressed by your self-confidence."

b) "And I bet you double or nothing he beats the pants off you."

c) "You should give him a handicap. You don't want to beat him too badly!"

He Says

1 Your girlfriend says the dreaded seven words: "Do I look fat in this dress?" Your answer is:

a) "I've been meaning to tell you, you look fat in everything."

b) "Actually, you look *phat* in that dress."

c) "No baby, it looks like you've *lost* weight." (Even though you suspect some seams might be busting at any moment.)

2 Your girlfriend shows up for school Monday morning, her beautiful blond hair newly died a shocking (and permanent) shade of pink. You hate it immediately, so you say:

a) "You look beautiful."

b) "It's very interesting!"

c) "What were you thinking?"

3 Your girlfriend has to give a speech in English class on the political allusions in Dante's *Inferno*. She begins with a lame attempt at humor: "Hades was really hot. How hot was it? It was so hot that even Beelzebub needed an air conditioner," and asks what you think of her opening. So you:

a) Shake your head and say, "Skip the joke, you're not very funny."

b) Howl with laughter like she's the next Janeane Garofalo.

c) Suggest she might want to begin such a weighty topic on a more serious note.

4 Your occasionally cute, occasionally annoying little sister, like the rest of the family, was not born with the gift of song. When she informs you she is going to try out for the lead role in the upcoming sixth-grade production of *West Side Story* you have to:

a) Tell her that she might want to reconsider and try out for the role of "2nd Girl in Dress Shop" instead.

b) Give the kid credit. She's got guts.

c) Tell her she's sure to win the role hands-down. Little Susie Temple just has no stage presence whatsoever.

5 Your g.f. buys her first car. She is totally psyched about it, but right away it's pretty obvious she's purchased a loser. When she asks you what you think of her new wheels you:

a) Say, "You'll look great in it—even when you're stuck in the breakdown lane."

b) Say nothing. You just grit your teeth each time the two of you have to hike two miles with a gas can because the gas gauge is broken.

c) Say, "I *warned* you not to buy a car from Larry's Lot o' Lemons. But did you listen? I think not."

6 Your dad loves to watch your chess matches. But lately he's taken to picking apart your every move on the ride home. Frankly, it's starting to wear you down. So the next time he starts criticizing your game, you say:

a) "Thanks, Dad."

b) "If you're so great, then how come you never won your high school tournament, huh?"

c) "Dad, it hurts my feelings when you criticize my game."

7 You're in art class, critiquing a fellow student's sculpture. It's obvious the kid just threw it together in the cafeteria, since it looks like a pile of garbage. Your teacher asks you to go first. You say:

a) "It's an um . . . interesting medium."
b) "It looks like a pile of garbage."
c) "It's a fascinating commentary on our disposable society."

SCORING:

1) a=3 b=2 c=1
2) a=1 b=2 c=3
3) a=3 b=1 c=2
4) a=3 b=2 c=1
5) a=2 b=1 c=3
6) a=1 b=3 c=2
7) a=2 b=3 c=1

If your score is:

17–21: BIG MOUTH.
Whew! Maybe you should take a deep breath and think about what you're going to say before you actually say it. You may tell yourself you're just being honest, but, hey, words can hurt! Is that really what you want?

12–16: FUTURE SPINMEISTER.
You know how to be tactful, and you have a way of looking at the bright side of things. That's great! And most times it's totally appropriate. You may occasionally have a tendency to avoid telling a painful truth. Some things need to get said—clearly.

7–11: SWEET NOTHINGS.
Your first impulse is to tell the other person something you think he/she would want to hear, true or false. Okay, it's hard to know when to tell the truth and when to tell a little white lie, but you could be giving people cavities with all the sugar-coating you've been doing. And remember—you're encouraging your sweetie to keep doing what you don't like. How smart is that?

Couples Quotient:

Yes, you do want to be spontaneous in a relationship, but you don't want to leave scars! Thoughtless remarks can wound—permanently, so couples who want to stay together would be wise to use some tact. Of course, that doesn't mean forgoing honesty. Personality comes into play, too—you have to know who you're dealing with. Two big mouths can get along fine—unless one of them is a *sensitive* big mouth! And sugar-coaters really have to watch it or they might end up in a totally fake relationship.

The Four Seasons

Everyone has a favorite season.
Do you two share the same one?
Take this quiz and find out!

You Say

1 Describe the perfect afternoon:
a) Strolling through the botanical gardens.
b) Lying on the beach, reading a mystery novel.
c) Playing Monopoly in front of a roaring fire.
b) Going apple-picking with your friends.

2 The sound most pleasing to you is:
a) The chirping of the first robin of the season.
b) The hum of cicadas.
c) Snow crunching underfoot.
d) Leaves crunching underfoot.

3 Your favorite sport is:
a) White-water rafting.
b) Water-skiing.
c) Skiing.
d) Hiking in the mountains.

4 The sight most beautiful to you is:
a) Flowers beginning to bloom.
b) The winking of fireflies.
c) The first snowflakes.
d) Leaves changing color.

5 Your favorite candy is:
a) Jellybeans.
b) Cotton candy.
c) Candy canes.
d) Candy corn.

42

6 Your favorite article of clothing is:
a) Anything pastel.
b) Your bikini.
c) Your reindeer hat and mittens.
d) Your flannel shirt.

7 Your favorite holiday is:
a) Easter/Passover.
b) Fourth of July.
c) Christmas/Hanukkah.
d) Thanksgiving.

He Says

1 Describe the perfect afternoon:
a) Strolling through the botanical gardens.
b) Lying on the beach, reading a mystery novel.
c) Playing Monopoly in front of a roaring fire.
b) Going apple-picking with your friends.

2 The sound most pleasing to you is:
a) The chirping of the first robin of the season.
b) The hum of cicadas.
c) Snow crunching underfoot.
d) Leaves crunching underfoot.

3 Your favorite sport is:
a) White-water rafting.
b) Water-skiing.
c) Skiing.
d) Hiking in the mountains.

4 The sight most beautiful to you is:
a) Flowers beginning to bloom.
b) The winking of fireflies.
c) The first snowflakes.
d) Leaves changing color.

Your favorite candy is:
a) Jellybeans.
b) Cotton candy.
c) Candy canes.
d) Candy corn.

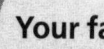 **Your favorite article of clothing is:**
a) Anything pastel.
b) Your surfer shorts.
c) Your wool hat and mittens.
d) Your flannel shirt.

Your favorite holiday is:
a) Easter/Passover.
b) Fourth of July.
c) Christmas/Hanukkah.
d) Thanksgiving.

SCORING:

If your answers are mostly A's:
Springtime is your season. The end of winter, the birds singing, the flowers blooming. You could very well be a warm, open person who is always looking for new possibilities.

If your answers are mostly B's:
You like it HOT! HOT! HOT! Fireworks, backyard barbecues, jumping the waves in the ocean, all are for you. Are you a passionate person who is free-spirited and ready to try new things at the drop of a hat?

If your answers are mostly C's:
Nippy winter nights, bundling up, snowshoeing, skating, and skiing all make you a happy person. You might love comfort, warmth, and feeling cozy.

If your answers are mostly D's:

Here are a few of your favorite things—brightly-hued trees, grinning jack-o'-lanterns, falling leaves. As a lover of fall, you may be a person who enjoys a bit of quiet and solitude, and is very creative.

Couples Quotient:

Okay, happy couples can find bliss together whatever the season. Still, a winter guy paired with a summer girl (or vice versa) could have trouble. You know, every July, Ms. Heat Miser wants to hit the beach while Mr. Cold Miser insists on air-conditioned comfort (if you can call 45 degrees comfort!). But really, it's not such a big deal, as far as problems go. And you can always learn to compromise! How about a day at the ocean and an evening at the movies? Sounds like fun!

The Ex-Factor

Everyone has a past.
But are you—or is he—
letting it threaten your relationship?

You Say

1 **How long did Crush Boy and his ex go out?**
a) Weeks.
b) Months.
c) Years.

2 **How long ago did he break up with his ex before you two started dating?**
a) One to three months.
b) Three to six months.
c) Two weeks or less.

3 **You are searching in his locker for your copy of *Of Mice and Men* when you unearth a tattered picture of the ex-g.f. When you show it to him, he:**
a) Looks surprised and says, "I thought I gave that back!"
b) Says, "Now where did that come from?" then erupts into nervous laughter.
c) Grabs it and says, "That's my personal property."

4 **The two of you are slow dancing at the Harvest Formal. You notice that the ex-girlfriend and her new beau just happen to be two couples away. Meanwhile, your guy:**
a) Is gazing into your eyes, totally oblivious.
b) Hisses in your ear, "Can you believe she's dancing this close to me! She's obviously obsessed!"
c) Appears to be boring holes into the back of her black taffeta frock with the sheer intensity of his stare.

5 Answer *always*, *sometimes*, or *never* to the following statements:

He slips up and calls you _____.
                                            (insert name of last girlfriend here)

He says, "_____ always used
              (insert name of last girlfriend here)
to . . ."

6 The last time he drove you home after school, you passed by her house. That's because:

a) He wanted to see if she was home, so he could get his CDs back from her.

b) He said he got lost.

c) She lives on your block.

7 You go to the diner together after school for a snack and she turns out to be your waitress. His reaction is one of:

a) Surprise. "She never used to work here on Fridays."

b) Glee. He changes his order several times and continually asks for weird condiments and stuff. "And what do you have in the way of chutney?"

c) Tension. He stammers as he places his order. "I'll have p-p-p-p-pastrami on p-p-p-p-pumpernickel, p-p-p-please."

8 True or false:
Her number's still on his speed dial.

9 When the two of you see her in the hallway, he:

a) Looks the other way.

b) Says hello and keeps going.

c) Starts a long and involved conversation, completely ignoring you.

He Says

1 How long did Crush Girl and her ex go out?

a) Weeks.

b) Months.
c) Years.

2 How long ago did she break up with her ex before you two started dating?
a) One to three months.
b) Three to six months.
c) Two weeks or less.

3 Your girlfriend asks you to look in her wallet for her library card. Behind her video membership card, you just happen to come upon her ex's class photo with a lovey-dovey message on the back. When you ask her about it, she:
a) Says, "Oops!" and tosses it in the circular file (that's the trash can).
b) Says, "Oh, isn't that odd"—though you notice she returns the photo to its plastic sleeve.
c) Wrests her wallet from your hands and says, "Who gave you permission to snoop in my personal belongings?"

4 The two of you are slow dancing at the Harvest Formal. You notice that the ex-boyfriend and his new babe just happen to be two couples away. Meanwhile, she:
a) Is gazing into your eyes, totally oblivious.
b) Hisses in your ear, "Can you believe he's dancing this close to me! He's obviously obsessed!"
c) Appears to be boring holes into the back of the ex's blue serge suit jacket with the sheer intensity of her stare.

5 Answer *always, sometimes,* or *never* to the following statements:
She slips up and calls you _____ .
(insert name of last boyfriend here)

She says, "_____ always
                    (insert name of last boyfriend here)
used to . . ."

6 The last time she drove you home after school you passed by his house. That's because:
a) She wanted to see if he was home, so she could get her CDs back from him.
b) She said she got lost.
c) He lives on your block.

7 You go to the diner together after school for a snack and he turns out to be your waiter. Her reaction is one of:
a) Surprise. "He never used to work here on Fridays."
b) Glee. She changes her order several times and continually asks for weird condiments and stuff. "And what do you have in the way of chutney?"
c) Tension. She stammers as she places her order. "I'll have p-p-p-p-pastrami on p-p-p-p-pumpernickel, p-p-p-please."

8 True or false:
His number's still on her speed dial.

9 When the two of you see him in the hallway, she:
a) Looks the other way.
b) Says hello and keeps going.
c) Starts a long and involved conversation, completely ignoring you.

SCORING:

1) a=1 b=2 c=3
2) a=2 b=1 c=3
3) a=1 b=2 c=3
4) a=1 b=2 c=3

5) always=2   sometimes=1   never=0
   always=2   sometimes=1   never=0
6) a=2   b=3   c=1
7) a=1   b=2   c=3
8) true=2   false=0
9) a=2   b=1   c=3

If your score is:

21–27: OBSESSION.

Hate to say it, but it sure seems like Loverboy/girl is carrying a torch for that old flame of his/hers! Maybe you two need to sit down for a little discussion. If his/her heart's not in the relationship, it's certainly not fair to you.

14–20: GONE BUT NOT FORGOTTEN.

Hmmm...there may still be a few embers burning. Probably the only thing you can do is play wait-and-see. But don't get all crazy and insecure or anything—that's a sure way to spoil a relationship.

7-13: IT'S OVER, OVER, OVER.

You can both relax. There's no life left in that old relationship. The ex is dead. Long live you!

Couples Quotient:

They say time heals all wounds. Or is it time wounds all heels? In any event, it takes most people a while to get over an ex. It's natural—you wouldn't want to go out with a serial dater, would you? But if the b.f. or g.f. takes things too far or drags things out for too long, it just might be time to say, "Sayonara, sweetie."

Are You a Material Girl?
Is He a Material Boy?

Where do your priorities lie?
How about his?
Do you dream of champagne and caviar?
Or diet soda and potato chips?
Take this quiz and find out how you
and your guy compare.

You Say

1 **For V-Day your coupled-up pals all get gifts made of precious metals from their "special friends." Your poor but well-meaning sweetie gives you a box of Cracker Jack with a plastic ring inside. When one of your friends shows you her 18K gold ankle bracelet engraved with the words "Together Forever" and asks what *you* got, you:**
a) Change the subject.
b) Say it's so expensive you don't dare wear it to school.
c) Proudly show off your gift. Mention that it's a snack and a piece of jewelry. *And* the ring's adjustable!

2 **Due to budgetary constraints at Yummy Yogurt, your boyfriend gets laid off. Now that only one of you is gainfully employed, movies and dinners at the Burger Barn are replaced by cable TV and leftovers. How do you feel?**
a) Resentful. You give him three weeks to find another job.
b) Sympathetic. You know how bad he must feel.
c) Resigned. You'll learn to love leftovers.

3 **Your great-aunt Mathilda is one crotchety old lady. Her Sunday visits make you wish the retirement village she lives in didn't allow its residents to roam at**

will. But you put up with her constant cheek pinching because:
a) She's old and you feel her pain.
b) Your mom makes you.
c) She gives big birthday checks.

4 You would be most bothered if your significant other took you out to dinner for your birthday and:
a) Took you to *his* favorite restaurant.
b) Left a lousy tip.
c) Didn't let you order the lobster-and-filet mignon special.

5 You would be most impressed if your boyfriend's folks:
a) Drove a really fancy car.
b) Had a well-stocked fridge.
c) Adopted stray dogs and found them new homes.

6 Loverboy writes you a personal in the school paper. It is a 20-line poem. You are touched because:
a) He found the time to write the poem even though he had a mid-term and a play-off game.
b) Personals cost 50 cents a line.
c) He somehow managed to find a word that rhymes with "Lollapalooza."

7 Your boyfriend gives you an old rhinestone brooch that once belonged to his grandmother. Tears fill your eyes because:
a) If it's a real antique, it could be worth big bucks!
b) You really don't like rhinestones.
c) You know how much he loved his grandma.

8 You are dying to go see the Smashing Pumpkins. The only seats the b.f. can get are nosebleeders. So you:
a) Are grateful because you know how he dialed his finger to the bone trying to get through.

b) Tell him never mind. You had your heart set on front-row seats.

c) Go along, but watch the whole show through the binoculars you borrowed from your bird-watching dad.

He Says

1 **All your friends get Tommy Hilfiger sweaters from their girlfriends for Christmas/Hanukkah. Your sweetie has a big family and is low on funds around the holidays, so you get a bargain-bin sweater. You:**
a) Wear it around the house when she comes over.
b) Return it and use the $12.99 credit toward some jumper cables.
c) Wear it proudly to school once a week. She picked it out for you; that's all that matters.

2 **Due to the rising costs of cottonseed oil at Corndog Palace, your girlfriend gets laid off. Now that only one of you is gainfully employed, movies and dinners at the Burger Barn are replaced by cable TV and leftovers. How do you feel?**
a) Resentful. You give her three weeks to find another job.
b) Sympathetic. You know how bad she must feel.
c) Resigned. You'll learn to love leftovers.

3 **Your great-aunt Mathilda is one crotchety old lady. Her Sunday visits make you wish the retirement village she lives in didn't allow its residents to roam at will. But you put up with her constant cheek pinching because:**
a) She's old and you feel her pain.
b) Your mom makes you.
c) She gives big birthday checks.

4 **You would be most bothered if your honey took you out to dinner for your birthday and:**
a) Took you to *her* favorite restaurant.

b) Left a lousy tip.

c) Didn't let you order the lobster-and-filet mignon special.

5 You would be most impressed if your girlfriend's folks:

a) Drove a really fancy car.

b) Had a well-stocked fridge.

c) Adopted stray dogs and found them new homes.

6 Your girlfriend writes you a personal in the school paper. It is a 20-line poem. You are most touched because:

a) She found the time to write the poem even though she had a mid-term and a play-off game.

b) Personals cost 50 cents a line.

c) She somehow managed to find a word that rhymes with "Lollapalooza."

7 Your girlfriend gives you her old baseball card collection because she knows you're a huge fan. Your first reaction is:

a) "I can't wait to get these home and see if there are any money-makers in here!"

b) "Cool! I love baseball cards!"

c) "You keep them. They could be valuable someday."

8 You are dying to go see Third Eye Blind. The only seats the g.f. can get are nosebleeders. So you:

a) Are grateful because you know how she dialed her finger to the bone trying to get through.

b) Tell her never mind. You had your heart set on front-row seats.

c) Go along, but watch the whole show through the binoculars you borrowed from your bird-watching dad.

SCORING:

1) a=2 b=3 c=1
2) a=3 b=1 c=2
3) a=1 b=2 c=3
4) a=2 b=1 c=3
5) a=3 b=2 c=1
6) a=1 b=3 c=2
7) a=3 b=2 c=1
8) a=1 b=3 c=2

If your score is:

20–24: MONEY MANIAC.

As that old '80s song (kinda) goes, "We are living in a material world, and you are a material person." It's hard for you to see beyond the monetary value in things.

13–19: MONEY MODERATE.

Let's put it this way: Money isn't the most important thing in your life, but if you found a suitcase full of cash you would most likely *not* take it to the nearest police station.

8–12: MONEY? WHO NEEDS IT?

You are not materialistic in the least!

Couples Quotient:

If the two of you are both up there on the materialism charts, you'd better hope for a high income or a lottery win. And if one of you is a Material Girl/Boy and the other is a more spiritual who-cares-about-cash type—beware! With such opposing attitudes, your relationship could end up bankrupt.

Can You Go With the Flow? Can He?

How do you react
when things don't go your way?
Do you throw a tantrum, or shrug and accept it?
What about your guy?

You Say

1 **For two months you've been planning to bring your main man to your family reunion and show him off to your "perfect" (that is, perfectly annoying) cousin. That morning his mom calls you up. He flipped his skateboard and broke his collarbone, and he's going nowhere. Your reaction?**
a) Why was that klutz taking risks the morning of my family reunion?
b) You're concerned about him, but a little upset you have to face your sarcastic cousin alone. "If you really have a boyfriend, then where is he? . . . Hmmm, a broken collarbone, how very convenient."
c) You assure him that of course it doesn't matter. His health is much more important than a silly family party. And now you won't have to worry about being embarrassed by your Uncle Ernie's incessant belching.

2 **You're at the movies and the film breaks mid-reel. Management gives you two free passes to make up for it. You:**
a) Feel gypped. Now you're going to have to sit through the entire first half again *and* buy a new tub of popcorn.
b) Feel like you won the movie lottery. Free tickets!
c) Say, "Whatever."

3 **You told your mom you'd go along with her to check**

out the new mall. After twenty minutes of circling an old cemetery, it's pretty obvious you're nowhere near the shoppers' paradise your mom lured you off the sofa with. You feel:

a) Curious. "Hey, since we're here, let's go check out the dates on some of those old tombstones."

b) Irritated. You want to go to the mall and you want to be there *now*.

c) Bored. You pull out the map, and soon you're on your way.

4 **You and your friends get the brilliant idea of spending the first crisp fall Sunday afternoon apple-picking. You'll meet at the orchard at noon. But when you arrive it's pretty apparent that *everyone* had the same brilliant idea. The place is mobbed, and you can't find your crew anywhere. So you:**

a) Search for your friends all afternoon. You find them at 3:55, five minutes before your mom arrives to pick you up.

b) Grab a bushel basket and start picking!

c) Call up your mother to come back and get you. This was a stupid idea anyway!

5 **Your parents inform you that the planned family trip to Hawaii has been changed to a trip to your Uncle Dudley's farm in Kansas. You are:**

a) Psyched. You've never seen an actual working pig farm before.

b) Understanding. The family funds must have been lower than expected.

c) Furious. "There's no way I'm going to Tornado Land for my summer vacation!"

6 **His mom insists you bring his little bro with you on your date to the drive-in. What's your reaction?**

a) You take along a lawn chair and a can of bug repellent

for little Georgie. He doesn't actually have to sit in the car with you, does he?

b) You call off the date.

c) You buy the little tyke a big bag of Swedish fish and welcome him aboard.

7 **When the sign-up sheet for speech topics circulates, you find that your perfect topic has been taken by someone else in your literature class. So you:**

a) Get into an argument with your classmate when she won't switch with you.

b) Shrug and choose a different topic. You'll make it great!

c) Grudgingly choose another topic. Next time you're getting the sign-up sheet first.

He Says

1 **Your photographer girlfriend promises she will take your picture for the yearbook candid page and have it developed in time for the deadline. But she never gets around to it. You are:**

a) Furious. If you can't have that pensive shot of you on the museum steps, you'd prefer nothing at all.

b) Indifferent. You rummage through your mom's photo albums for a suitable photo.

c) Inspired. You run to the arcade photo booth to get a strip of photos of you making funny faces.

2 **The night before your ten-page paper on Newton is due your dinosaur of a computer crashes, taking all the changes you made since you last saved two hours ago. You:**

a) Test the laws of gravity by throwing your monitor out your bedroom window.

b) Take a deep breath and a ten-minute TV break.

c) Scream.

3 You are out on a first date in your sister's ancient convertible VW bug. You go to the drive-in, top down, and are immediately set upon by a swarm of blood-sucking mosquitoes. By the time you hand-crank the top back up, the car is filled with the little parasites. You:

a) Spend the rest of the double feature taking turns squashing the skeeters and laughing. This is one first date neither of you will forget!

b) Lose your cool and head straight home, cursing the whole way.

c) Start the car and drive to the nearest air-conditioned multiplex.

4 You plan to meet some friends at the wave pool at H_2O Heaven, the local waterslide park. But the place is mobbed, and you can't find them anywhere. So you:

a) Search for your friends all afternoon. You find them at 4:55, five minutes before the park closes.

b) Change into your trunks. It's hot out and you're getting wet!

c) Go home. It was a stupid idea anyway!

5 Your parents inform you that the planned family trip to Hawaii has been changed to a trip to your Uncle Dudley's farm in Kansas. You are:

a) Psyched. You've never seen an actual pig farm before.

b) Understanding. The family funds must have been lower than expected.

c) Furious. "There's no way I'm going to spend my summer vacation in Tornado Land!"

6 The g.f. has been grounded and won't be able to go to the Star Trek convention you two have been planning on attending for months. Your reaction is to:

a) Be disappointed, but try not to make her feel guilty.

b) Get into a big argument with her parents. The nerve of them—making such a big deal out of her failing two subjects in one semester!

c) Take your Trekkie friend instead and buy your little Spockette a pair of Vulcan ears to cheer her up.

7 When the sign-up sheet for speech topics circulates, you find that your perfect topic has been taken by someone else in your literature class. So you:

a) Get into an argument with your classmate when she won't switch with you.

b) Shrug and choose a different topic. You'll make it great!

c) Grudgingly choose another topic. Next time you're getting the sign-up sheet first.

SCORING

1) a=3 b=2 c=1
2) a=3 b=1 c=2
3) a=1 b=3 c=2
4) a=2 b=1 c=3
5) a=1 b=2 c=3
6) a=2 b=3 c=1
7) a=3 b=1 c=2

If your score is:

17–21: SHORT FUSE.
Whoa! It doesn't take a lot to set you off. Maybe you should try meditation. Or medication? Really, try not to take things so hard! Sometimes it's not what happens that's important, but the way you look at it.

12–16: LONG FUSE.
Most of the time you take life's ups and downs like a pro. But every now and then, when you're pushed too far, you do get mad. And then, watch out!

7–11: FUSE-LESS.

Bravo! You're always turning broken eggs into omelets and generally making the best of things. Just make sure to be sympathetic to those not blessed with your cheerful and sunny outlook.

Couples Quotient:

If a match of extremes is going to work long term, it will usually be the mellow one who is responsible. She/he can bring some sanity to the proceedings! But what about two people with short fuses? There's just no telling—but be prepared for fireworks!

How Social Are You?
How Social Is He?

Are you both social butterflies?
Or lone wolves?
And can a butterfly and a wolf
somehow make a fine match?

You Say

1 Your parents are out of town for the weekend. Your little brother's at Grandma's. You decide it's the perfect night to:
a) Soak uninterrupted in a nice hot bath.
b) Invite your best friend over to watch a movie.
c) Invite 50 of your closest friends over for a little "study session."

2 Time to Free Word Associate. When you hear the word PARTY, the first word that pops into your mind is:
a) HAT.
b) MESS.
c) TONIGHT.

3 You're offered the lead in the school play. You take it because:
a) You hear the cast party is rockin'.
b) Your mother has been pressuring you to turn off your computer and make some friends.
c) You feel you were born to be on stage.

4 Where do you sit in the caf?
a) With your friends.
b) Wherever you please; you have friends everywhere.
c) Alone.

5 **You identify most with:**
a) Batman and Robin.
b) The Lone Ranger.
c) The cast of *Friends*.

6 **Your favorite part of a party is:**
a) Saying good night.
b) The planning.
c) The mingling.

7 **What's your general attitude toward friends?**
a) Can't have too many.
b) Quality not quantity.
c) Who needs 'em?

8 **Double dates are:**
a) Double the fun.
b) Worse than acne.
c) Fine once in a while.

9 **Your motto is:**
a) The cheese stands alone.
b) The more the merrier.
c) Two's company.

He Says

1 **Your parents are out of town for the weekend. Your little brother's at Grandma's. You decide it's the perfect night to:**
a) Finish that model airplane you've been working on.
b) Invite your best buddy over to watch a movie.
c) Invite 50 of your closest friends over for a little "study session."

2 **Time to Free Word Associate. When you hear the word PARTY, the first word that pops into your mind is:**

a) HAT.
b) MESS.
c) TONIGHT.

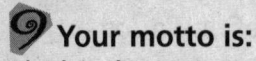 **You're offered the lead in the school play. You take it because:**
a) You hear the cast party is rockin'.
b) Your mother has been pressuring you to turn off your computer and make some friends.
c) You feel you were born to be on stage.

Where do you sit in the caf?
a) With your friends.
b) Wherever you please; you have friends everywhere.
c) Alone.

You identify most with:
a) Batman and Robin.
b) The Lone Ranger.
c) The cast of *Friends*.

Your favorite part of a party is:
a) Saying good night.
b) The planning.
c) The mingling.

What's your general attitude toward friends?
a) Can't have too many.
b) Quality not quantity.
c) Who needs 'em?

Double dates are:
a) Double the fun.
b) Worse than acne.
c) Fine once in a while.

Your motto is:
a) The cheese stands alone.

b) The more the merrier.
c) Two's company.

SCORING:

1) a=1 b=2 c=3
2) a=2 b=1 c=3
3) a=3 b=1 c=2
4) a=2 b=3 c=1
5) a=2 b=1 c=3
6) a=1 b=2 c=3
7) a=3 b=2 c=1
8) a=3 b=1 c=2
9) a=1 b=3 c=2

If your score is:

22–27: PAR-TAY!

You're probably never happier than when you're in a crowd. Admit it—just thinking about socializing gets you going, doesn't it?

15–21: SOCIABLE, NOT SOCIAL.

You enjoy spending time with a group, but you can miss a big bash without batting an eyelash. Probably your favorite kind of socializing is one-on-one.

9–14: ME, MYSELF, AND I.

You really like your own company. Good for you! You might want to try to get out a little more, though!

Couples Quotient:

Heads up! A big difference in this area can be a relationship breaker. A solitary kind of person and a social kind of person need to do a lot of adjusting. Maybe you'll want to schedule time apart so you can each satisfy your socialization (or lack thereof) needs.

Are You a Private Person?
Is He?

Is there a lock on your diary?
A sign on your bedroom door that says "KEEP OUT"?
Or do you have a free-to-be-you-and-me attitude?

You Say

1 **You're on the phone. When you hang up, your mom asks who you were talking to, so you:**
a) Sit down at the kitchen table and give her a blow-by-blow of your friend Carmen's boyfriend woes.
b) Tell her, "Carmen."
c) Groan and say, "Mom! I don't ask you who you're talking to. Well, not all the time, anyway."

2 **The rule with your little sister about your room is:**
a) Knock first, please.
b) No entrance without an appointment. Your door is always locked.
c) You have an open-door policy.

3 **Your best friend spots your display of Sweet Sixteen birthday cards in your bedroom and picks one up to read, so:**
a) You grab it from her hand, saying, "Do you mind?"
b) It's no big deal. If they were personal, they wouldn't be out on display.
c) You're a little bothered that she didn't ask first.

4 **You are daydreaming, and your boyfriend asks what you are thinking about, so you:**
a) Get defensive. "What are you, the thought police?"
b) Filter. "Nothing interesting."
c) Tell him. "Well, I was wondering what would happen if

I were cloned. Would I be able to beat myself in checkers, or would it always be a tie?"

5 **You're at home with the flu. The boyfriend calls to see how you're feeling. You give him:**
a) The *Reader's Digest* condensed version. "Not so good, sweetie."
b) The silent treatment. "Some things are personal, you know."
c) The unabridged version. "Man, I have never puked so much in my life!"

6 **Where do you have most of your phone conversations?**
a) Sitting in the middle of the family room.
b) Locked in the hall closet.
c) It depends on the nature of the call and the gender of the caller.

7 **You get into a fight with your mom. The next day you're in a bad mood. One of your friends asks you what's wrong, so you say:**
a) "Just a little family disagreement."
b) "Well, my mother said I could borrow her earrings if I asked first, so she wasn't home, but I asked once before and I didn't wear them, so I figured I had a leftover permission, so I borrowed them. Well, who would have figured I'd knock them down the drain . . ."
c) Nothing.

He Says

1 **When you come home from school, your mom asks how your day was. You say:**
a) "Well, let me tell you," and give her a blow-by-blow, including your choices at lunch.
b) "Fine. I got a 99 on my math test."

67

c) "Mom! You're always so nosy!"

2 Your g.f. asks to keep her sneakers in your locker, which is conveniently located near the gym, so you:
a) Give her your combo, warning her about your sweaty gym socks.
b) Meet her at your locker before and after gym class so that you can take out and put back her sneaks.
c) Subdivide the locker, clearing out a special section for her.

3 You and your friend come home and you want to listen to your phone messages. What do you do?
a) Wait until he goes home.
b) Play them.
c) Ask him to leave the room.

4 Your girlfriend asks you about your first kiss. So you say:
a) "That's between me and Sally Peterson, my kindergarten girlfriend."
b) "I was five."
c) "Well, we were sitting in the doll corner, eating milk and cookies when it happened. I was wearing my Health-Tex corduroys and little Sally had on this red jumper. We both reached for the Ernie doll and . . . hey, are you paying attention?"

5 You are sitting in the middle of the school bus telling your buddy about your date Friday night when you realize that several sets of ears are listening. You immediately:
a) Lower your voice and tell the rest of your story.
b) Clam up—and say you'll finish the conversation in homeroom.
c) Raise your voice so even the bus driver knows you went

to the Rollodrome with the cutest girl in the tenth grade.

6 Where do you keep cards and other personal stuff from your girlfriend?
a) On your desk.
b) In a locked box at the top of your closet.
c) In a drawer.

7 You are writing a poem to your beloved. You look up to find your dad reading it over your shoulder. He says, "That's pretty good, son," and you:
a) Are a little embarrassed, but pleased he likes it.
b) Ask him to sit down and help you out with that tricky rhyming couplet at the end.
c) Slam your notebook shut and say, "Do you mind?"

SCORING:
1) a=1 b=2 c=3
2) a=2 b=3 c=1
3) a=3 b=1 c=2
4) a=3 b=2 c=1
5) a=2 b=3 c=1
6) a=1 b=3 c=2
7) a=2 b=1 c=3

If your score is:

17–21: PRACTICALLY PARANOID.
Are you planning on a career in the CIA or something? You're throwing up all kinds of barriers between you and the rest of the world. Stop and think—don't you feel closest to the people who share their thoughts and feelings? Try and relax a little.

12–16: NOT PARTICULARLY PRIVATE.
You're not about to open up to just anybody, but you're reasonably trusting. There are things—passionate love letters, for instance—that you probably do keep to yourself. But no double

locks or booby traps for you. You assume people are not going to poke and pry into your personal life without an invitation.

7–11: PRIVATE? PUH-LEEZE!
Talk about trusting! You're probably ready to tell your life story to whomever sits next to you on the bus. It's great to be open. But you may want to be more selective about who you share with. And remember, even your closest buddies may not want *all* the details!

Couples Quotient:
Privacy can be a major issue for a couple. One person can feel left out while the other feels crowded. And also, a sharer may disclose something to a friend or family member that the other half of the couple feels is absolutely sacred. Proceed with caution! But if both halves of the couple take each other's feelings about this V.I.I. (Very Important Issue) into consideration, it just might work.

How Old Is Your/His Inner Child?

Are you fifteen going on forty,
or fifteen going on four?
Are you impulsive . . . or deliberate?
Take this quiz and find out!

You Say

1 On your way home from school you pass a neighbor's lawn sprinkler. You:
a) Cross the street. You don't want to get water spots on your Air Walkers.
b) Well, it depends on how hot it is.
c) Time it for optimal soaking. Whee!

2 Your friend Becky calls you at 8:00, Friday night, with two tickets to see a band you kinda like. She'll be by to pick you up in ten minutes. You say:
a) "Tell me again who the warm-up band is?"
b) "Hello? I already took out my contacts! The only groups I'm watching are on MTV."
c) "I'll clear it with the parental units and see ya in ten minutes!"

3 Say you want to go. What's your approach with the people who give permission. (That would be your parents.)
a) "I really, really, really want to go. I'll do the dishes for a month. Please, please, please, please, please. Pretty please."
b) "I'm going to a concert with Becky. Don't wait up."
c) "I know it's last minute, but Becky just got tickets to see this great band. I won't be out too late. Would it be okay if I went?"

4 **How do you feel about spur-of-the-moment activities?**
a) They have their time and place.
b) I avoid them at all costs.
c) Anytime, anyplace, anywhere. I'm ready.

5 **You're at the school dance and no one's dancing. The DJ asks you what song will get you and everyone else moving. You pick:**
a) A lovely waltz.
b) The Hokey Pokey. You're the first one up there putting your right hand in.
c) A retro dance tune from the 80s. *We Got the Beat*!

6 **The class prez tells you the girl who usually plays the school mascot is sick. Can you fill in?**
a) Oh, I don't know. It'll get so hot and stuffy in that penguin suit.
b) If word gets out that it's me waddling around out there on the basketball court, I'll never be able to show my face in homeroom again.
c) This is the moment I've been waiting for! I'll be the best darn penguin ever!

7 **Your friend is standing right at the edge of the pool, talking to her secret crush. Do you have an urge to push her in?**
a) Oh yes! And it will be even better if she pulls him in with her.
b) No—that would be a very immature thing to do.
c) After I check to see if she's wearing her new sunglasses. If not, she's in.

8 **Your friend is getting dressed after gym class, and you notice that her skirt is tucked into her underwear. You:**

a) Walk by and yank it out for her.

b) Grab your hairbrush like a microphone and sing, "I see London, I see France, I see Kirsten's underpants!"

c) Whisper in her ear about the little problem.

9 On weekends you never miss:

a) *Saturday Night Live.*

b) *The MacNeill/Lehrer Report.*

c) Saturday morning cartoons.

10 Free Word Association time. When you hear the word MUD you immediately think:

a) PIE.

b) PUDDLE.

c) PACK.

He Says

1 On your way home from school, you pass a neighbor's lawn sprinkler. You:

a) Cross the street. You don't want to get water spots on your Air Walkers.

b) Well, it depends on how hot it is.

c) Time it for optimal soaking. Whee!

2 Your friend Danny calls you at 8:00, Friday night, with two tickets to see a band you kinda like. He'll be by to pick you up in ten minutes. You say:

a) "Tell me again who the warm-up band is?"

b) "Hello? I already took out my contacts! The only groups I'm watching are on MTV."

c) "I'll clear it with parental units and see ya in ten minutes!"

3 Say you want to go. What's your approach with the people who give permission. (That would be your parents.)

a) "I really, really, really want to go. I'll do the dishes for a month. Please, please, please, please, please. Pretty please."

b) "I'm going to a concert with Danny tonight. Don't wait up."

c) "I know it's last minute, but Danny just got tickets to see this great band. I won't be out too late. Would it be okay if I went?"

4 How do you feel about spur-of-the-moment activities?

a) They have their time and place.

b) I avoid them at all costs.

c) Anytime, anyplace, anywhere. I'm ready.

5 You're at the school dance and no one's dancing. The DJ asks you what song will get you and everyone else moving. You pick:

a) A lovely waltz.

b) The Hokey Pokey. You're the first one up there putting your right hand in.

c) A retro dance tune from the 80s. *We Got the Beat*!

6 You're hanging out with your friend while she spins disks at the school radio station. Suddenly there's a crisis—the CD player starts skipping and your friend begs you to fill the dead air while she fixes it. So you:

a) Pick up your copy of *War and Peace* and start reading.

b) Start a call-in show. Hanson: Musical geniuses or musical misfits?

c) Start doing your Donald Duck impressions.

7 Your friend is standing at the edge of the pool, chatting up a lifeguard, when you get the urge to push him in. Do you do it?

a) But of course. And it will be even better if he does a belly-flop and soaks the lifeguard.

b) No—the pool rules clearly state: NO HORSEPLAY.

c) Only after making sure he's standing at the deep end.

8 Your friend is just about to ask the girl of his dreams out on a date. Do you go with your instinct to yell, "Hey, studly, I like the outfit your mom picked out for you today!"?

a) I do, but I know that he would kill me, so I refrain.

b) I don't just have the urge, I follow through.

c) No—that would be a very childish and inappropriate thing to do.

9 On weekends you never miss:

a) *Saturday Night Live.*

b) *The MacNeill/Lehrer Report.*

c) Saturday morning cartoons.

10 Free Word Association time. When you hear the word MUD you immediately think:

a) PIE.

b) PUDDLE.

c) SEASON.

SCORING:

1) a=1 b=2 c=3

2) a=2 b=1 c=3

3) a=3 b=2 c=1

4) a=2 b=1 c=3

5) a=1 b=3 c=2

6) a=1 b=2 c=3

7) a=3 b=1 c=2

8) a=2 b=3 c=1

9) a=2 b=1 c=3

10) a=3 b=2 c=1

If your score is:

24–30: Your inner child is SIX.
As far as you're concerned, there's no age limit on trick-or-treating or merry-go-round rides. That makes you fun to be around. Of course, there are times (finals week, for example) when you need to ground your inner child.

17–23: Your inner child is SIXTEEN.
You can make adult-style decisions and still pull a crazy practical joke or enjoy some spontaneous kid-type fun. Impressive!

10–16: Your inner child is NINETY-SIX.
Take it easy, there. You wouldn't want to excite yourself or anything! Sad to say, you seem to have a senior citizen's outlook on life. True, maturity is a big plus a lot of the time, but you might enjoy cutting loose now and then.

Couples Quotient:
As long as both partners appreciate each other's qualities, most any combo can work, even a NINETY-SIX paired with a SIX. The half with the younger outlook on life can insert a little free-wheeling fun into the festivities, and teach the other to live a little! And the half with the older outlook can keep track of all the boring stuff—like due dates, deadlines, and curfews. It might just be a winning combination!

What's Your PDA (Public Display of Affection) I.Q.? And His?

There are two schools of thought on
Public Displays of Affection.
To some, they're perfectly acceptable;
to others, they're perfectly awful.
Where do you and Loverboy/girl stand?

You Say

1 What's the most appropriate way for a boyfriend and a girlfriend to say hello to each other?
a) An oral exam.
b) A quick kiss.
c) A handshake.

2 At parties the two of you can be found:
a) Holding hands.
b) Making out in the corner.
c) Hanging out on opposite sides of the room.

3 How do you feel about walking down the hallway with your arms around each other?
a) It's okay, as long as the halls are deserted.
b) I would hate to risk having my arm fall asleep and not be able to take notes in class.
c) Yeah, baby!

4 Hands in each other's back pockets is:
a) Très tacky.
b) The absolute best way to perambulate.
c) Not for me unless we're looking for spare change.

5 After boarding your respective school busses, you

bid your sweetie farewell by calling out the bus window:
a) "I miss you already!"
b) "Call me tonight!"
c) "See you later, alligator!"

6 Your boyfriend comes off the soccer field complaining of a twisted knee, so you:
a) Cover it with kisses, then ask, "All better now, honey?"
b) Run off to get an ice pack.
c) Say, "No pain, no gain."

7 You run into your boyfriend's dad at the supermarket, so you give him:
a) A big smile.
b) A nod. (Hey, he's not *your* dad.)
c) A huge hug and a kiss on the cheek.

He Says

1 What's the most appropriate way for a boyfriend and a girlfriend to say hello to each other?
a) An oral exam.
b) A quick kiss.
c) A handshake.

2 At parties the two of you can be found:
a) Holding hands.
b) Making out in the corner.
c) Hanging out on opposite sides of the room.

3 How do you feel about walking down the hallway with your arms around each other?
a) It's okay, as long as the halls are deserted.
b) I would hate to risk having my arm fall asleep and not be able to take notes in class.
c) Yeah, baby!

4 **Hands in each other's back pockets is:**
a) Très tacky.
b) The absolute best way to perambulate.
c) Not for me unless we're looking for spare change.

5 **After boarding your respective school busses, you bid your sweetie farewell by calling out the bus window:**
a) "I miss you already!"
b) "Call me tonight!"
c) "See you later, alligator!"

6 **The bell rings and your sweetie comes bursting out of Spanish class, devastated by the F she's just received on a test. You:**
a) Kiss away her tears.
b) Offer a comforting hug in the middle of the hallway.
c) Buck her up with your patented pick-me-up speech. "When the going gets tough, the tough get going . . ."

7 **You run into your girlfriend's mom at the supermarket, so you give her:**
a) A big smile.
b) A nod. (Hey, she's not *your* mom.)
c) A huge hug and a kiss on the cheek.

SCORING:

1) a=3 b=2 c=1
2) a=2 b=3 c=1
3) a=2 b=1 c=3
4) a=1 b=3 c=2
5) a=3 b=2 c=1
6) a=3 b=2 c=1
7) a=2 b=1 c=3

If your score is:

17–21: PUBLICLY PASSIONATE.
No one would call you guys inhibited! You're probably the envy of many, so have some pity on those less passionate, less demonstrative, less in love (not to mention those with a lower PDA tolerance) and tone it down a little.

12–16: TRADITIONALLY TOLERANT.
You won't recoil at a public kiss or hug, but you're not likely to play it hot and heavy in front of an audience. Basically, you're fine with public displays of affection, it's P.D.P.s (Public Displays of Passion) that give you pause.

7–11: A LITTLE PRIVACY, PLEASE.
The public could easily mistake you and your honey for mere acquaintances. But don't worry, it's the private displays of affection that really count!

Couples Quotient:
Of course, couples with similar PDA I.Q.s will do just fine. But what if one half of the couple loves to show the whole world just how much he/she cares while the other prefers public restraint? How's this for a compromise—SPDAs (*Sneaky* Public Displays of Affection)? Secret love notes, knowing glances, holding hands under the lunchroom table . . . the possibilities are endless!